It's My Birthday!

MARIA HOSKINS

ILLUSTRATED BY

NECLA YILDIRIM UNAL

It's My Birthday! by Maria Hoskins
Published by C&V 4 Seasons Publishing Co.
© Copyright 2023

ISBN: 978-1-7358388-1-6 | Hardback
ISBN: 978-1-7358388-2-3 | Paperback
Library of Congress Control Number: 2022919263

Cataloging-in-Publication data

Names: Hoskins, Maria, author. | Unal, Necla Yildirim, illustrator.
Title: It's My Birthday! / by Maria Hoskins; illustrated by Necla Yildirim Unal.
Description: Arkansas: C&V 4 Seasons Publishing, 2023. | Summary: Archie plans a fun birthday for himself.
Identifiers: LCCN: 2022919263 | ISBN: 978-1-7358388-1-6
Subjects: LCSH Birthdays--Juvenile fiction. | Family--Juvenile fiction. | Zoos--Juvenile fiction. | Parties--
Juvenile fiction. | BISAC JUVENILE FICTION / General
Classification: LCC PZ7.1 .H67 It 2023 | DDC [E]--dc23

Illustrations by Necla Yildirim Unal
Edited by Rose Williams
www.seasons2dream.com

It's My Birthday
is dedicated to my
husband, Archie, and
father to Christina and
Victoria. Thank you for
being our living example
on how to share your
time, life, and love.

Today is a very special day!
It's My Birthday!

My family, and all my classmates,
will celebrate my special day,
In a delightful and exciting way!

Come join us and you will see,
All the super duper fun it will be.

There will be
food, fun, games,
and an activity,
And all of it has
been planned by me.

First, I'm helping my mom cook my favorite breakfast. Pancakes with bananas and strawberries, topped with whipped cream! There's bacon and sausage too! Yummy, yummy, I love my mommy!

ow we're off to have a fun-filled day.
ere comes the big yellow school bus,
pick up my family and friends.
's Zoo Day, and we're on our way!

So many animals to see,
giraffes, lions, a zebra,
an elephant, and a bear.
Animals must be kept safe,
so we'll make a donation,
because we care.

Let's form teams. On the **C Team** are Christina, Connor, Camie and Cathy; Jose, Javier, Jamal and Joan make up the **J Team**; the **K Team** has Kendra, Kiki, Kelly and Kevin; and the **V Team** rounds up with Victoria, Victor, Viney and Vanessa. With your team, let's ride the merry-go-round. Up and down, up and down and round and round.

It's now time for my
favorite game, the Piñata!
Come teams, put on the
blindfold and take a turn.
Whoop, swoop, slam, bam!
Jose gotta the piñata!

On to the park for lunch and birthday cake! Wow!
White icing, colorful sprinkles, candy balloons, and
big letters that spell "Happy Birthday" on a giant cake!
Come on everyone, let's eat cake! Hurry, don't be late!

It has been a super duper, jolly whooper, fun-filled birthday celebration! I am so happy that my family, friends, and classmates joined me for my special day. Oh, one last thing to do before our return bus ride home.

There is a table covered in prettily wrapped birthday presents, topped with big colorful bows, purple, green, pink, yellow, orange, red, blue, silver, and gold. Surprise everyone! A present for me and a present for each of you too!

My birthday holiday
was the best ever!
Let's swoop, dup,
alley oop! And, let's
do it again next year!

My Birthday is:

Month: _____

Date: _____

Year: _____

Add a picture:

Write a story
"For my birthday, I would like to......"

_____

_____

_____

_____

_____

Add a picture or draw illustrations

Color the balloons

Color your Birthday Cake

CPSIA information can be obtained
at www.ICGtesting.com
Printed in the USA
LVHW071243180723
752702LV00007B/12